CW00729701

SPOT
The Prisoner

Home Farm Twins

Spot

The Prisoner

Jenny Oldfield

Illustrated by Kate Aldous

Hodder
Children's
Books

a division of Hodder Headline plc

With special thanks to the pupils of Brookfield Primary School, Mickleover.

Copyright © 1999 Jenny Oldfield
Illustrations copyright © 1999 Kate Aldous

First published in Great Britain in 1999
by Hodder Children's Books

The right of Jenny Oldfield to be identified as the Author of
this Work has been asserted by her in accordance with the
Copyright, Designs and Patents Act 1988.

10 9 8 7 6 5 4 3 2 1

All rights reserved. No part of this publication may be
reproduced, stored in a retrieval system, or transmitted,
in any form or by any means without the prior written
permission of the publisher, nor be otherwise circulated
in any form of binding or cover other than that in which
it is published and without a similar condition being
imposed on the subsequent purchaser.

All characters in this publication are fictitious and any resemblance
to real persons, living or dead, is purely coincidental.

A Catalogue record for this book is available from the British Library

ISBN 0 340 72796 9

Typeset by Avon Dataset Ltd, Bidford-on-Avon, Warks

Printed and bound in Great Britain by
The Guernsey Press Co. Ltd, Channel Isles

Hodder Children's Books
a division of Hodder Headline plc
338 Euston Road
London NW1 3BH

One

'I wannabe . . . I wannabe rich, like Laura Saunders!' Helen Moore chanted. She'd invented a game as she walked along the shore of the lake with her twin sister, Hannah. Laura was their wealthy friend who lived at Doveton Manor. 'I wannabe . . . famous, like, like, like . . .' She paused to think of her favourite pop singer or soccer star.

'Like Black Beauty and Lassie!' Hannah threw a stick for their dog, Speckle. He chased it into the lake, then swam back with it.

'No, stupid. It has to be a *person*!' Helen called it the "Wannabe Game". You had to choose three

things you wanted to be when you grew up and find
an example of someone you admired. 'Famous, like
Madonna.'

'What football team does he play for then?' Hannah
quipped, then wrestled the wet stick from Speckle's
mouth.

'Never mind!' Helen sighed and walked on. It was
late September, the leaves on the chestnut trees at
the water's edge had turned bright yellow and red.
'And last of all I wannabe . . .'

'. . . Happy?' Hannah suggested the third thing.

'Yeah, of course; happy.' Helen scoffed at her
sister's idea. 'If I'm rich and famous, obviously I'm
going to be happy!'

'Not *nec-ess-ess-air-ri-ly*!' Hannah stumbled over
the long word. She launched the stick back into the
clear, cold water. 'I know loads of rich and famous
people who aren't happy.'

'Like who, for instance?' Helen was ready for a
good argument, until she spied something that stole
her attention. It was a Dalmatian puppy bowling
along the pebble beach towards them. He wagged
his tail, yelped at Speckle and begged to join in the
fun.

'Like . . . some lottery winners. Like the woman who lives at Hazelwood.' Hannah found an example right under their noses. She pointed to a large house half-hidden behind tall trees. The house was old and very grand, overlooking the lake. It had the best view in Doveton. 'Mrs *Whatsername*, the artist woman.' Hearing the puppy bark, Hannah turned to watch him bound along the beach. 'She must have loads of money to live in a house like that, and she's a famous painter because even Dad says he's heard of her. But every time you see her in the village, she looks dead miserable.' It was a long speech to prove her point, but Hannah might as well have saved her breath.

'Aah, look!' Helen ignored her. She squatted on her haunches to greet the black-and-white spotted dog. 'Look at his floppy ears! Look at his shiny black nose! Look at his cute little pink paws!'

The puppy leaped into Helen's arms then squiggled and squirmed. He licked her hands with his rough tongue.

'Where's his owner?' Hannah felt a twinge of jealousy. She wanted to be the one whose hands the sweet spotty dog was licking.

'Hey, yes!' Helen rubbed him and patted him.

She squeezed and cuddled him. '*Yessy-wessy, who's looking after you, you sweetie-weetie ickle fing!*'

'Yuck!' Hannah shuddered, then scanned the shore. There were upturned rowing-boats by the jetty, and three white swans were gliding by on the smooth, silvery water. 'Listen, Helen, there doesn't seem to be anyone around.'

'Maybe he's lost.' Helen held him up in the air, letting his stumpy legs dangle. She pursed her lips and made tweeting sounds. '*Are you losty-wost, you poor fing?*'

'Try reading the disc on his collar,' Hannah suggested coolly. She felt Helen was going a teenie bit over-the-top as far as the spotted puppy was concerned. She reached down to stroke Speckle. Their very own Border collie sat obediently to heel, stick in mouth, brown eyes twinkling at the excitable new arrival.

'Now, let me read your name and address,' Helen began.

The puppy squirmed as she reached for his red collar. He jumped free and landed on all fours.

'Quick, catch him again!' Hannah gasped.

Speckle stood up and wagged the white tip of his tail.

As the puppy shook his head, his black ears flopped and flapped. He yapped excitedly.

'Go on, catch him!' Hannah urged.

Helen made a dive for the dog. He jumped sideways to start a play-fight with the Border collie. Helen landed on her stomach and grabbed a handful of pebbles. '*You* catch him!' she grunted.

So Hannah did her best. She tried to grab the puppy as he sat on his haunches and boxed Speckle with his front paws. He darted out of reach. Then she chased him in circles, and zig-zagged after him down the beach to the water's edge.

'Watch out!' Helen warned. The puppy had charged into the water, right across the path of the three gliding swans. He splashed as he galloped, yapping wildly, then suddenly yelping as he ran out of his depth.

'Oh no!' Helen followed Hannah to the edge of the lake. She put a hand over her eyes, afraid to watch.

'He's sinking!' Hannah saw the little black-and-white head vanish below the surface. 'No, he's not; he's come back up . . . he's floating . . . he's beginning to do doggy-paddle!'

The puppy kept his nose above water as the swans, at first surprised, then irritated, by the disturbance, surrounded him. They raised their huge white wings and beat the air, showering downy feathers on to the calm water.

'Uh-oh!' Helen knew what swans were like when they got angry. They would hiss and snake their long necks, and poke the poor puppy with their pointed yellow beaks.

Hannah glanced down at Speckle, waiting eagerly by her side. He looked back up at her for instructions.

'Fetch!' Hannah gave the order. 'Go on, Speckle, bring the puppy back here!'

The Border collie sprang to the rescue without a second's delay. He swam straight and true, between two of the swans, ducking their beating wings and reaching out to grab the puppy by the scruff of its neck.

'Excellent!' Helen cried, as their dog turned for the shore. The three swans lost interest and sailed majestically on their way. Speckle towed the puppy to safety. 'Brilliant, Speckle. You saved us from getting wet!'

He reached the pebbles and dropped the bedraggled puppy. Down went the two dogs' heads, as they began to waggle and shake themselves dry.

'Uh-oh-oh-ooohh! You spoke too soon!' Hannah and Helen were soaked to the skin.

'Great!' Helen muttered. She stared down at her splattered sweatshirt and jeans, leaving Hannah to grab the puppy at last. 'So, what does it say on his name-tag anyway?'

Hannah read the engraved words. 'His name's "Spot",' she announced.

'Very original,' Helen muttered. 'And where does he live?'

Tucking the wet puppy under her arm so that she could hold him still and read on, Hannah frowned and glanced up the shore at the grand house hidden behind the trees. 'It says "Hazelwood",' she murmured. Then she re-read the whole disc. ' "Spot. Hazelwood, Lakeside, Doveton." '

'So he's not really lost after all.' Helen too stared up at the tall, white house. It was built on a hill, surrounded by high walls and bushes designed to keep strangers out. Big, stained-glass windows overlooked the lake. For all they knew, Spot's owner could have stood at one and watched the whole waterworld adventure.

Hannah looked down at the wet puppy and tickled him under the chin. He ducked his head and licked her fingers. 'Well,' she sighed, squaring her shoulders and facing the facts. 'Before you catch your death of cold or get up to any more mischief, I guess we'd better take you home!'

'Home' for Spot was through some tall wooden gates, up a steep drive. There were thick laurel bushes growing at either side, a damp smell of earth and wet leaves, dark shadows creeping down a sloping lawn, a squirrel sprinting across it and . . . silence.

Helen reached up and lifted the heavy lion's-head knocker. *Rat-tat-tat!*

The twins waited with Spot and Speckle. No answer.

Helen rapped the panelled oak door a second time.

'It's no good, there's no one in,' Hannah decided. Still keeping a tight hold of the runaway puppy, she stepped back to look up at the tall, arched windows.

'It looks more like a church than a house,' she whispered.

'Or a prison.' Helen frowned at the iron studs in the heavy door, then tried the knocker one more time.

'Fancy living here . . . !'

'. . . Alone!'

'. . . With no one to talk to!' Hannah knew the rumours about Hazelwood; that the artist who lived here had no family and never had visitors. You sometimes saw her in Luke Martin's village shop, buttoned up inside an old grey overcoat, her long grey hair escaping from a silver clasp. She would be buying milk or posting letters, but she never talked; not even to say hello.

'Creepy!' Helen shivered. 'Shut away in some old studio with her paint-brushes and oil paints and stuff!' She took a sharp intake of breath as, inside the house, a door banged. 'Shh, she's coming after all!'

Hannah listened hard. Safe in her arms, Spot cocked one floppy ear.

They waited again. No footsteps. More silence.

'Maybe it was a ghost!' Helen giggled nervously.

Hannah didn't appreciate the feeble joke. 'So what are we going to do now?' she asked, as she wandered back down the drive to get a better view of the whole house. 'We can't just leave Spot to run loose in the garden, can we?'

'No. He'll only escape again.' Helen pointed to the open gates and the gaps in the rose hedges to either side. 'And there's a busy road between here and the lake. He could easily get run over!'

'You know something; there are bits of the house separate from the main part.' Hannah pointed to a row of old outbuildings across the yard that might once have been stables. These days, to judge by the rusty handles and hinges and the cobwebs across the small windows, it looked as if no one used them. But at right-angles to the stables, overlooking the lake, was a newer, more modern building with big windows. The white door stood open and the evening sun shone in.

'Tut!' Helen realised they'd been wasting their time. She gave up on the main house and set off quickly across the yard. 'That's where Spot's owner must be!'

It seemed that Spot agreed. With a sudden squirm

and a twist, he jumped from Hannah's arms. He ran to overtake Helen, yapping and swerving in through the open door.

Helen stopped and waited for Hannah and Speckle to join her. 'That's that, then.' Spot had obviously discovered his owner.

'Hadn't we better check?' Inching forward to crane her neck around the door, Hannah peered inside.

The big, barn-like room smelled of paint. There were artists' canvases propped against the wall, easels, boxes, chairs and step-ladders in a jumble to one side. And there was Spot racing around under the chairs, his high-pitched bark echoing in the huge space.

'Wow!' Helen whispered. This was nothing like their orderly art room at school. There was a giant piece of driftwood in one corner, rescued from the shore of the lake; chunks of interesting-shaped rock – even the skulls and bones of animals lined up on a shelf.

'Yes?' a voice said from behind.

The twins spun round, hearts thumping. They recognised the thin, wispy-haired figure of the lonely painter. She wore an old white shirt smeared with paint and carried a clutch of long, thin brushes in one hand. Her dark eyes glared at them from a lined, severe face, eyebrows knotted, the corners of her mouth turned down in grim lines.

'We . . . er . . .' Hannah stammered.

'We found your puppy by the lake!' Helen did better at gasping out an explanation.

The woman's eyes flicked from Helen's face to Hannah's, then down at Speckle. 'I want you to leave my property,' she told them, pushing past Helen. She stood in front of a large painting of mountains and lakes, making it clear that she didn't want them to see it. 'I don't allow anyone in my studio.'

'We're very sorry!' Helen and Hannah mumbled their apology, backing out of the doorway into the shadowy yard. They swallowed hard, feeling somehow as if they'd committed a major crime.

'And please close the gate as you leave.' Spot's owner followed them to the door and watched them coldly down the drive.

'It was open when we c-ca . . .' Helen began. But Hannah jabbed her with her elbow.

'Never mind.' Hannah swung the gates shut. She

saw Spot emerge from the studio, a bundle of black-and-white energy, racing down the drive. The gates slammed just in time to stop him from running out after them.

From the entrance to her precious studio, the artist watched in stern silence.

'Stay!' Hannah urged the puppy.

He jumped up at the gate, poking his black nose through the gaps. He whined and whimpered to be allowed to play.

'Yes, stay!' Helen frowned up the hill at his rude owner. The miserable woman hadn't even bothered to say thank you to them for bringing Spot home.

Instead, she stared angrily at them, her dark brows knitted, her eyes full of suspicion.

What on earth was the matter with her? What did she think they'd done wrong?

'Come on!' Hannah said to Helen and Speckle. Though she still felt sorry for little Spot, wagging his tail and wanting to play, she knew she'd had enough of spooky Hazelwood for one day. 'For goodness sake, let's get out of here!'

Two

'That puppy's lonely!' Helen plunged dirty dishes into the bowl and frothed up the soap suds. All during their evening meal, the twins had described the problem to their mum and dad.

Hannah cleared the table. 'He's a prisoner in that big, horrible house!' she declared.

'Now, girls, there's no need to exaggerate.' Mary Moore tried to calm them down while their dad went to answer the door. 'Don't let the fact that you're mad keen on anything with four legs cloud your judgment more than usual,' she warned them. 'The puppy is probably very well cared for, and just

15

because you don't like his owner doesn't mean you have to rush off to the RSPCA to report her for cruelty!'

'B-but . . . ! Helen began. 'It wasn't just Mrs *Thingummy* . . .'

'. . . It was the house!' Hannah jumped in. 'Hazelwood is dead spooky. Honest, Mum, it makes those little hairs at the back of your neck stand up on end just looking at it!'

'Mrs *Thingummy*? Hazelwood?' A visitor sauntered into the kitchen and immediately tuned in to what they were saying. 'You must mean Marilyn Higham, the world-famous animal artist.'

'Luke!' Helen dropped the dish she was holding into the water. There was a tidal wave of suds over the sides of the bowl. 'Tell Mum and Dad how nasty she is. Go on, tell them!'

But before the village shopkeeper could answer, Hannah jumped in. 'Animal artist?' she echoed in surprise. 'You mean, Mrs High-wotsits paints pictures of *animals*?'

'Marilyn Higham.' Luke repeated the name. 'Yes, and she's very good at it. She's travelled all over the world to study animals in their natural habitat. Africa and India. Her paintings of lions and elephants are amazing.'

'I've seen a few printed in wildlife magazines,' David Moore agreed. 'Those paintings are so realistic you'd think they were photographs until you look really closely.'

'Hmm.' Hannah chewed her bottom lip. 'You'd think that would mean she liked animals . . .'

'And doesn't she?' Luke sat at the kitchen table and made himself at home. He took a mug of coffee from Mary, stroked Socks, the Moores' tabby cat, and prepared to listen.

'She's got this puppy . . .' Hannah began.

'. . . A black-and-white spotty dog. He's only a few months old,' Helen went on.

'She let him run around near a busy road!' Hannah told him.

'And never even said thank you when we took him back!' Helen declared.

'Now, girls, I've already told you to mind your own business.' Their mum gave them a warning look.

'That's right.' Their dad finished the job of clearing the table for Hannah. 'From what Luke says, you've no need to worry about the puppy.'

'Tell them, Luke!' Mary turned to him. 'Prove to them that Marilyn Higham isn't the Wicked Witch of the East!'

Luke rubbed his dark beard and winked at the twins. 'Well, let's see, where shall I begin? Marilyn Higham is the daughter of Sir Charles Higham—'

'Who's he?' Helen interrupted.

'Give me a chance. Sir Charles Higham was an important artist of the forties and fifties. He made his name by painting factory scenes and city streets. The family moved to Hazelwood forty years ago. Marilyn must have been in her twenties then, and she'd just married Michael Wood . . .'

'Who's he?' Hannah quizzed.

'He was . . . you guessed it . . . another artist! His thing was natural scenery; the mountains and lakes around Doveton and Nesfield mainly. Marilyn and Michael stayed on in the house when Sir Charles died. They had one son, Simon.'

'Don't tell me, yet another artist?' Helen cut in.

Luke grinned and nodded.

'That's funny, I had the impression that Mrs Higham didn't have any family,' David Moore said thoughtfully. 'You never see anyone except her coming and going from that enormous house.'

'Here comes the sad bit,' Luke explained. 'Michael Wood died five years ago, quite suddenly, I seem to recall. Marilyn was devastated. After his death she hardly ever went out. Apparently the house is full of her husband's paintings, a sort of gallery to celebrate his life and work. She hasn't touched a thing in his part of the studio either. His paint-brushes and canvases are still in exactly the place where he left them; his last finished work is still propped against the wall.'

'Uh!' Helen thought this was creepy.

'That *is* quite sad!' Hannah sighed.

'Yes, but the worst part was that Marilyn and her son, Simon, fell out over Michael's will. No one quite knows why, but it means that Simon never sees his mother now. She cut him off and refuses to let him visit Hazelwood, though he only lives nearby; in Nesfield, as a matter of fact.'

'She never sees him?' Mary asked. 'It must have been one *ser-i-ous* row!'

Luke shrugged. 'Simon's married with children of his own, and apparently Marilyn Higham has never seen her grandchildren.'

'She's become a kind of recluse,' Mary murmured.

'A what?' Helen and Hannah asked.

'A recluse. Someone who doesn't go out,' their dad explained. 'They stay shut up inside their houses, cut off from everyone and everything.'

'See, I said she wasn't happy!' Hannah reminded Helen. She stood at the window looking out into the farmyard at the Home Farm geese and chickens, at Solo their pony peering out over his stable door and Speckle rooting amongst the fallen leaves and conker shells that had fallen from the horse-chestnut tree.

'Hazelwood is like a posh prison,' Helen pointed out. 'Not just for her, but for Spot as well.'

'Helen!' Mary warned.

'Hannah!' David guessed what his soft-hearted daughter might be thinking.

'But Spot needs a friend!' Hannah cried. Now that Luke had told them Mrs Higham's story, she knew this more than ever. The friendly little puppy didn't deserve to be cooped up at Hazelwood with no one to play with.

'Someone to go for walks with,' Helen agreed. 'Someone to run along the beach with and go for swims with.' She came to the window and stood beside Hannah, staring out at the geese and the hens, and at Speckle seizing a stick and trotting across the yard with it.

'Spot needs someone older, who would teach him tricks and look after him.' Hannah had made up her mind by the time Speckle pushed at the door with his front paw and came into the kitchen.

Helen gazed down at their Border collie. A smile crept on to her face; her dark brown eyes lit up with what she thought was a brilliant idea.

Ignoring their mum and dad's advice about minding their own business, the plan was already hatching as they turned the dog around and sneaked outside with him. He dropped the stick for Hannah to pick up, cocked his head to one side, and waited for the throw.

She stooped, gathered the stick, and prepared to fling it over the wall into the adjoining field. 'What Spot needs is a friend like you, Speckle!' she confided.

'Good old, reliable, sensible, clever, brilliant you!' Helen agreed.

'Not so much of the old, eh, Speckle?' Hannah

launched the stick. 'Reliable? Yes. Sensible and clever? Naturally. Brilliant? You bet!'

The twins smiled as the dog raced after the stick. He bounded across the yard, scattering chickens in his path. Then he was over the wall and out of sight.

' "*Walkin' the dawg, boom-boom-boom,*
  Just a-walkin' the dawg!" '

David Moore sang the twins on their way. He was loading bakers' trays into the car, which was parked outside the kitchen door, ready to drive the twins' mum into Nesfield for a busy Saturday in the cafe.

'Here, Speckle; here, boy!' Helen called. She swung the lead and gave a long, shrill whistle.

' "*If ya don't know how to do it,*
  I'll show ya how to walk the dawg!" '

Speckle scampered through the crisp fallen leaves which blew across the farmyard. He sat for Helen to put on his lead.

' "*Chagga-chagga-boom!*" ' Their dad did dance steps around the car.

'*You're* in a good mood.' Mary appeared at the door dressed for work in neat black trousers and a white shirt. Her dark hair was clasped back from her face and she carried the last full tray of home-baked biscuits for the cafe.

'And why not?' David gave her a breezy smile. 'Today's the last cricket match of the season, and I reckon Luke and I picked a pretty good team last night.'

Mary sniffed. 'It keeps you out of mischief, I suppose.' She glanced at the twins, who were heading for the gate with Speckle in tow. 'Talking of mischief . . . What are you two up to today?'

Hannah and Helen picked up speed. They turned down the lane towards the village.

'We're walkin' the *dawg*!' Helen called over her shoulder.

'Well, don't be long. Tell your dad what time you'll be back. Keep out of trouble!' Mary issued last-minute instructions.

'As if!' Hannah raised her eyebrows and sighed.

' "*Just-a walkin' the dawg*," ' their dad crooned, his voice drifting down the lane. ' "*Boom-chagga-boom!*" '

' "And today our new dog-walking route takes us down Doveton Fell, along the shores of beautiful

23

Lake Doveton!" ' Helen pinched her nose and pretended to be a tour-guide. ' "Visitors to the area will notice ye ancient wooden jetty where ye quaint steamboat ferry picks up and drops off ye passengers. And, set back from the lake, is ye magnificent home of ye very ancient, famous local artist!" '

Hannah giggled as she took Speckle's lead from Helen. Then she suddenly grew serious. Now that Hazelwood was in view, she'd begun to have second thoughts about their plan. 'What if Mrs Higham is looking out of her window?' she asked.

Helen led the way up the beach and across the winding road. She marched boldly up to the closed gates of the house. 'We're not breaking any law,' she insisted. 'We're standing by the road. If anybody asks, we just happened to be passing by!'

'What if Spot isn't here?' Hannah still held Speckle on the lead. She wouldn't let him off until they spied the lonely puppy.

'He is.' Certain that their idea would work, Helen began to scout along the rose hedge for gaps that a Border collie could creep through. 'And if Spot can't come out to play because his owner's too mean to take him for walks, who's to say that he can't invite another dog in?'

Hannah watched Helen crouch down beside a suitable gap in the prickly hedge. She let Speckle lead her to the place and sniff at the damp grass, while all the time keeping a wary lookout across the sloping lawn towards the tall, silent house. The wide front door was firmly closed as before, and the wind whistled through the trees on the hill, whirling dead leaves across the courtyard.

'Here comes Spot now!' Helen saw the puppy first.

He flew around a corner, ears flapping, clumsy feet falling over one another in his rush to greet them. Half-galloping, half-tumbling and rolling, he careered across the lawn.

'Hello, little Spot!' Helen knelt and peered through the hedge. 'Here's Speckle. He's come to play!'

The puppy yapped and flung himself at the rose bush. He yelped and fell back as a sharp thorn pricked him.

'No, wait,' Helen tried to explain. 'You can't come out, so Speckle is going to creep through to join you.' She shuffled to one side to give the Border collie room. 'Go ahead,' she whispered.

Speckle cocked a questioning ear. It wasn't normal for the twins to order him into someone else's neatly-kept garden.

'Go on, it's OK!' Helen gave him a small, helping shove. 'Just for a few minutes. We'll keep a lookout!'

So Speckle crouched low and crept through the gap in the hedge. An excited Spot jumped on top of him and rolled over and over, grappling his new playmate and play-fighting across the lawn.

'Aah!' Helen sat back on her haunches and smiled. She felt a warm glow at a good deed well done. This was just how it should be; a young puppy playing with an older dog, learning lots of important things about how to behave.

'Speckle's very patient!' Hannah whispered. She relaxed and squatted beside Helen for a better view. 'It's probably because he's used to Socks crawling over him and nicking space in his basket at home.'

'And Spot loves it!' Helen watched the puppy break away from Speckle and run circles around him. Then he bounded back and wrestled him again.

They were congratulating themselves, planning

daily visits with Speckle, forgetting to keep a proper lookout, when suddenly the front door of the house opened.

'Shoo!' Mrs Higham strode down the lawn, sweeping-brush in hand. She was pale and angry-looking, dressed in the same paint-covered shirt as before, her hair escaping from its clasp and flying about her thin face. Coming between Spot and Speckle, she thrust the broom against Speckle's side and pushed him over.

'Hey!' On the far side of the hedge, Helen sprang to her feet.

'Go away; shoo!' The artist shoved the broom into Speckle's face.

'Stop!' Hannah pleaded. She saw Speckle cower away from the stiff bristles of the brush, heard him yelp in pained surprise.

Mrs Higham poked and pushed their dog back towards the hedge. 'I know who you are and what you want!' As Speckle scuttled through the thorny gap, she shot the twins a furious glance.

'We . . . we were just taking Speckle for a w-walk!' Helen protested.

The old woman tossed her head. 'You would do better not to walk him this way in future!' she insisted. 'This is my property and you must not encourage your dog to trespass again . . . yes, *encourage*!' she repeated, her intense dark eyes boring right through Helen.

'W-we're sorry!' Hannah gasped. She put Speckle on the lead and pulled him away from the hedge.

Mrs Higham threw down the broom and scooped Spot up from the ground. 'You will be!' she hissed, turning from them and striding up the lawn. 'If you so much as come near my dog again, you will be very sorry indeed!'

Three

'I thought Mrs Higham was going to really whack Speckle with the broom!' Helen relived the event next day for the benefit of Laura Saunders. She, Hannah and Laura were leaning on the fence of Sultan's paddock, watching the chestnut thoroughbred bicker with Scott and Heather, Laura's new Shetland ponies. The big horse chased the little piebalds from the best patch of grass, tossing his dark mane and swishing his long black tail.

'I've never met her,' Laura told them. 'My parents bought one of her paintings once. I think they even asked her if she would do a portrait of Sultan for us, but from what I remember she wasn't interested.'

'I bet she was rude,' Hannah said. 'She wouldn't just say no politely; she'd probably shout and take a broom to them and rush them off her precious property!'

'Dunno.' Laura was more interested in how Scott and Heather were settling in at Doveton Manor than in hearing about a nutty old lady. 'But she can't be all that mean. Our gardener, Mark, is over at Hazelwood doing some work for her today. She rang him last night and promised to pay him double his normal rate if he came right away.'

Helen frowned. Generosity didn't seem to be Mrs Higham's usual line. 'What kind of work?'

'Dunno. Gardening, I expect.'

Hannah pictured the garden of the grand house. The neat lawn and trimmed laurel hedges hadn't looked as if they needed Mark's urgent attention. She glanced at Helen and saw that she too was puzzled.

'I think we'd better go!' Helen said suddenly, as if she'd just remembered something they had to do.

'Yep! Bye, Laura. See you later!' For once, Hannah lost interest in the horses and followed Helen down the drive.

Laura dragged her attention away from sturdy little Scott and dainty Heather. 'Was it something I said?' she called.

But the twins were already too far away to hear, running for the manor gates, turning down the road that led to the lake.

'Just a little look!' Helen promised.

'Yes. We can see all we want to see by standing on the beach,' Hannah agreed. 'The house is on a hill, so we can look at the garden from a long way off.'

Helen's feet crunched over the flat pebbles by the water's edge. Sunday was a busy day for trippers, but few ventured this far out of the village on foot. Most preferred a ride in one of the old-fashioned steamboats that chugged across the calm, clear lake, giving them a good view of the fells beyond. 'So we won't be anywhere near Mrs Higham's P-R-O-P-E-R-T-Y!' she scoffed. 'Yet we'll still be able to see what Mark's doing.'

'The point is, Luke told us last night that Mrs Higham's practically a recluse.' Hannah thought out loud as Hazelwood came into view in the distance.

'She hardly ever goes out and she never has visitors. So how come she suddenly invited Mark to go and do some work?'

'Yeah, and what was so urgent?' Helen went on. Her suspicions grew as they drew nearer to the house. She could see Mark's blue van parked by the gates, but no sign so far of the slight, fair-haired figure of the Saunders' young gardener.

'Well, he's not mowing the lawn.' Helen stopped by the jetty and scanned the sloping garden. 'And he's not trimming the laurel bushes . . .'

'No, there he is, by the front door!' Hannah pointed him out at last. She'd spotted him standing there in a green polo shirt and jeans, obviously talking to Mrs Higham, whose scrawny, dishevelled figure was not on view. When the door closed, Mark put something in his pocket and walked down the drive towards the gate.

'Quick!' Helen made a run from the beach to the road to intercept the gardener's van. They reached it just in time to flag him down.

'Where's the fire?' Mark had recognised the twins and wound his window down.

'No fire!' Helen gasped. 'We wanted to know what

you were doing at Mrs Higham's, that's all.'

'I was helping her out with a little job,' came the reply. 'Why?'

'What job? That's the point!' Hannah squinted along the road, trying to see past Mrs Higham's garden gates. 'Digging? Pruning?'

Mark gave a short, puzzled laugh. Glancing ahead, he caught sight of a car coming along the single-track road. 'You're weird, you two,' he told them, easing his van forward. 'But if you must know, I've been putting up a fence for the old dear.'

'A fence?' the twins echoed.

'Yeah. You know; concrete posts in the ground, wire-netting. That kind of fence.'

For a few metres, Helen and Hannah ran along the grass verge, beside Mark's van. 'What for?' Hannah asked. 'Why did she want a fence?'

'To stop her puppy from getting out,' he told them, gathering speed and giving them a farewell wave. 'And to stop other dogs getting in, apparently!'

He was gone. A black car was coming slowly towards them, passing them as they stood open-mouthed. It stopped at the gates of Hazelwood.

'Now Spot really *is* trapped inside that garden!'

Helen breathed. She crept along the road towards the garden. And yes, she could see it now; a high wire fence newly erected behind the rose hedge, taller than she was.

'He's a prisoner!' Hannah said quietly. 'It's not fair. She never comes out to take him for proper walks and she won't let him talk to other dogs either.'

'Poor Spot, he's in *wotsit*-confinement!' Now Helen didn't care whether or not Mrs Higham saw her. She marched right up to the black car as a youngish, dark-haired man got out and tried the gate.

'Solitary,' Hannah told her. She went and pressed her nose against the shiny new fence. 'It's called solitary confinement. That's how they punish really bad people in prison, and, can you believe it, Helen, it's actually happening to Spot!'

The driver of the black car had opened the gate and walked up the drive before Hannah and Helen had got over their dismay. He looked up at the windows of the main house, then knocked at the door.

From the gate, the twins watched the man wait. And wait. 'Why doesn't she answer?' Helen muttered. 'We know she's in there, so why doesn't she come to the door?'

The man knocked again. He stood hands in pockets, deep in thought. Then he stepped back from the house, craned his neck towards the upper storeys and called out in a loud voice. 'Mother?'

'It's the son from Nesfield!' Hannah was surprised because Luke had told them that Marilyn Higham had cut Simon off and refused to let him visit.

Helen nodded. 'He looks like her. Well, a younger version. He's got the same eyes.'

'I never noticed his eyes,' Hannah admitted. In any case, there was no doubt about it. 'Mother' was what he'd shouted.

'Mother, answer the door!' the visitor called again. 'Please!'

In one of the upstairs windows, Hannah and Helen saw a curtain move. Or could it have been a reflection of the nearby trees moving in the breeze?

'It's Simon!' the man called. 'I need to speak to you. Please, Mother!'

There was no reply. The door stayed firmly shut.

'That's so mean!' Helen muttered. 'She must have heard him.'

'Shh!' Hannah strained to listen. If she tried hard, she thought she could hear the sound of a high, muffled bark. 'That's Spot!' she hissed.

Simon Higham must have heard it too. He went up the stone steps and peered through the letter-box. The noise of barking grew louder, then faint again as he let go of the flap and the box closed. Shaking his head, the man drew a white envelope from his pocket, looked at it for a long time as if in doubt, then quickly pushed it through the letter-box. He turned and half-ran down the drive, and for the first time took notice of the twins standing there.

'That was probably a bad idea,' he told them hurriedly, though he'd never seen them in his life before. He seemed flustered and upset. 'She'll most likely tear it up without opening it.'

'Hum.' Hannah shuffled uncomfortably. She stared down at her trainers. Grown-ups didn't usually confess things to kids they'd never met.

Helen was bolder. 'Why won't Mrs Higham read the letter?' she asked.

The son glanced back at the silent house. 'Because . . . oh, reasons.' He shrugged. 'A hundred reasons; don't ask me. It's funny . . .'

'What is?' Helen closed her ears to the sound of Spot barking from behind the closed door. She concentrated instead on what Simon Higham might be doing here.

'Not funny; strange. It's strange to think that I lived here for most of my life. I know every inch of that house and studio, every tree in the garden, I saw that view of the lake every time I looked out of my bedroom window.' He gazed thoughtfully down the hill.

'And now she won't even answer the door,' Helen said quietly. Yes; that *was* really weird.

Simon took a sharp breath that seemed to catch in his throat. 'I don't know why I even bother!'

Blushing, still embarrassed by his confessions to strangers, Hannah glanced back at the house. There was movement at the window; this time she was sure it wasn't a reflection. It was a figure watching them. 'Hang on!' she cried.

But it was too late. Mrs Higham's son had got into his car and slammed it into gear. He was reversing on to the road, revving the engine, drowning the sound of Hannah's voice.

Hannah pointed to the window where the figure stood. 'Try again! Your mother's in there, but maybe she didn't hear you!'

The black car crunched over gravel on the hard shoulder, its wheels skidded, then it sped away.

Sighing, Helen turned to study the woman at the window. The face was pale and expressionless, the hand holding back the curtain was steady as she stared down at them.

'She heard,' Helen muttered under her breath as she turned away from the house in disgust. 'Definitely! No; she's just a mean, spiteful old woman who won't even open the door to her own son!'

Four

For days Helen and Hannah tried hard not to think about poor Spot.

'There's no point you worrying yourselves to death over him,' their dad had told them. 'Since there's nothing you can do, the best thing is to put it to the back of your minds and get on with the rest of your lives!'

So they'd ridden Solo out on Doveton Fell every day after school, trotting the grey pony up the mountain, along heather-bordered bridleways. Speckle had come too. But when Hannah had picked up a stick for him to fetch and she'd watched him race across the hillside, the wind ruffling his shiny black coat, the tip of his white tail weaving between rocks and bushes, she'd thought of the Dalmatian pup shut away behind the new wire fence. Then she'd sighed and gone home feeling sadder than ever.

And when Helen had done her morning chores of feeding Sugar and Spice, the Home Farm rabbits, and Lucy and Dandy, the Home Farm geese, she'd been reminded of how great it was to have a farmyard full of animals; how Speckle and Socks and Solo had each other for company, and how Spot at Hazelwood had no one . . .

'There's still nothing you can do,' Mary Moore told them at the end of the week. It was Friday night in early October. Leaves spiralled from the tree in the farmyard. As Helen swept with the giant outdoor broom and Hannah piled the leaves on to a bonfire in the corner, yet more blew down to take their place. 'Your dad was right, girls. You must mind your own business and leave Mrs Higham to look after Spot as she sees fit.'

'But we heard him crying!' Helen protested.

'When?' Mary frowned.

'This afternoon. On our way home from school.

We . . . kind of . . . came a different way back for a change.'

'Hmm. And it just happened to take you along Lakeside, past Hazelwood?' Their mum shook her dark hair free from its clasp, then buttoned up her jacket.

'It was really sad.' Hannah gathered up an armful of dead leaves. 'Spot had his nose pressed up against the fence. As soon as he saw us he recognised us and started to cry.'

Mary gave her shoulder a squeeze. 'Sorry, love!' she whispered. Then, more briskly, 'But you know the answer: come home from school the normal way in future, and steer well clear of Mrs Higham's house.'

Hannah lay in bed that night smelling the bonfire smoke in her hair and staring out of the tiny window at the wind chasing silver-edged clouds across the moon.

'Hann?' Helen whispered. It was past midnight. 'Are you asleep?'

'No.'

'Me neither. Guess who I'm thinking about.'

'Spot.'

'Yep. How about you?'

'The same.' Hannah admitted that no way could she follow their mum and dad's advice. There was a long silence as they remembered Spot's face behind the fence: a sad, lonely black-and-white face with deep, dark eyes. 'Helen?' she murmured.

'Yeah, I'm still awake. I was wondering: do you think we could . . . kind of . . . help Spot to escape?'

Hannah sat up in bed. 'You mean, sort of cut a hole in the fence and let him out? Then kind of hide him somewhere for a bit until Mrs Higham forgets about him?'

'Is that what you were wondering too?' Helen could only see the pale blob of Hannah's face across the dark room. 'Don't you think it's a great idea?'

'Maybe.' Hannah was cautious. 'But it'd be kidnapping, wouldn't it?'

'*Dog*-napping, more like.'

'Yeah, dog-napping.' Hannah refused to be thrown off-course. 'Where would we hide him for a start? And what would we do with him in the end?'

'Find him a good home.' Helen had already worked this bit out. 'There must be loads of people who'd want to adopt a sweet little Dalmatian pup!'

'But where would we hide him?' Hannah returned to the hard part. Half of her wanted to agree to the plan, but half of her was scared.

'I don't know yet, do I?' Huffily Helen turned her back. 'Do I have to think of every single thing?'

'I suppose we could hide him in a barn somewhere,' Hannah said slowly. There were plenty of old stone buildings belonging to the farms on Doveton Fell. 'Say, John Fox's or Fred Hunt's – or Sam Lawson's at Crackpot Farm . . .' Sam was their friend from school.

Eagerly Helen turned back to face Hannah. 'No, not Sam's place. Sam would be bound to find out, and you know he could never keep his mouth shut. I think Fred's barn would be better!' High Hartwell Farm was next to theirs. They would easily be able to keep an eye on Spot if they hid him there. 'So when do we do it?' she pressed Hannah.

Hannah swallowed hard. They'd need wire-cutters to cut through the fence. They'd have to make sure that Spot was in the garden and choose part of the fence that was out of sight of the house. 'This weekend,' she whispered.

'Tomorrow morning!' Helen decided.

Thick clouds drifted across the mooon, the room grew darker. 'Helen?' Hannah whispered after a long silence.

No answer. There was heavy, regular breathing from the other bed.

'You're sure we're not over-reacting?' Hannah said. Wire-cutters and dog-napping: these were risky things. But then she thought of Spot's lonely, whimpering cry. 'No, I guess not!'

With a sigh, she lay down to try to get some sleep.

Helen's mouth was dry, her stomach tied in knots. It was one thing talking about dog-napping Spot, quite another thing when it came to doing it. In her jacket pocket she carried a heavy pair of wire-cutters which they'd secretly taken from their dad's tool-box. They bumped against her leg as she walked, and made a big bulge. She felt certain that everyone was looking at her and wondering what it was.

'Hang on a sec; my lace is undone!' Hannah stopped outside Mr Winter's house on Doveton High Street. Her hands were shaking with fear as she stooped to tie it.

Helen waited. Then they walked on together towards Luke's shop.

'Hi, Hannah! Hi, Helen!' Laura Saunders cycled by.

They jumped guiltily. 'Oh, er, hi, Laura!'

Their friend cast them a quizzical look and pedalled on.

'Wotcha! What are you two up to?' Sam Lawson leaped out of Luke's doorway to make them jump.

'N-nothing!' Helen stuttered. 'Go away, Sam!'

'Oh, very nice!' He blocked their way, pretending to be offended. ' "Go away, Sam!" That's very nice, that is!'

Hannah side-stepped to get past, up into Luke's shop doorway, narrowly avoiding bumping into a customer who stood just inside the door.

'You can leave your parcel on the counter, Mrs Higham,' Luke was saying as Hannah turned to say sorry.

She gasped and froze. Behind her, Helen crept on to the doorstep to take a look.

'Here, let me help.' Luke came from behind his post-office counter to take a large, flat, square package from Marilyn Higham. 'It's the wrong shape to put on the ordinary scales,' he explained. 'I'll have to weigh it specially and then put the correct stamps on for you.'

'Take care, it's fragile!' The elderly artist snapped at the shopkeeper. She had her back to the twins and so far she hadn't noticed them.

'Come on, let's get out of here!' Helen whispered.

Hannah edged back. It was just their luck to run into the owner of Hazelwood at the very moment when they planned to steal her dog. Still, if they hurried ahead, it would mean that the house would be empty and they would have a

good chance to carry out their secret plan.

'Hey!' Sam's loud voice made Luke and Mrs Higham look round. 'You two girls look like you're up to something!'

'Oh no!' Helen groaned as Mrs Higham fixed them with a haughty stare. She trod hard on Sam's foot.

'Ouch!' He hopped dramatically through the door and fell on to a chair inside the shop. 'What did you go and do that for, Helen Moore?'

'Shh!' Hannah begged. So much for their hope of creeping off unnoticed.

'Erm, this parcel's going to be rather expensive to send, I'm afraid.' Luke did his best to ignore the interruption. 'Especially if we make it Recorded Delivery.'

'Never mind. I don't care what it costs. When will it arrive at its destination?'

'Let's see now. It's a Nesfield address. Today's Saturday, so we should be able to guarantee delivery on Monday morning.'

Mrs Higham pressed her thin lips together. 'That will have to do. I'm leaving later today, so I must trust the Post Office to do its job.'

'Leaving?' Luke made polite conversation as he

lifted and weighed the package. 'Does that mean you're deserting us in Doveton for a while?'

The old lady nodded briefly. 'I'm shutting up Hazelwood for the winter and going to stay in Italy.'

'Very nice too.' Luke tore strips of stamps from his book, licked them and stuck them to the parcel. 'Lucky for some, eh?' he said to Sam and the twins.

Helen's eyebrows shot up. She stared at Hannah. *Italy? The house all locked up until spring?*

'What about Spot?' Hannah mouthed silently back.

'I suppose that'll mean putting your little dog into kennels while you're away,' Luke went on. 'Of course, it's the one disadvantage of having a pet: what to do with it while you're away.'

The twins saw the back of Mrs Higham's neck stiffen. Her voice was raised to a brittle pitch as she answered.

'As a matter of fact, I don't have the puppy any more,' she told Luke loud and clear.

'No?' The shopkeeper glanced at Helen and Hannah. The look said, Listen to this!

'No. He was a nuisance. Always whining and under my feet when I was trying to work. So I decided to get rid of him.'

Stunned, Hannah collapsed on to a chair next to Sam. Helen's mouth fell open. What did she mean, *get rid of him*!

Taking money for the stamps from Mrs Higham, Luke tried to look as if he understood her decision. 'And when did that happen?' he asked.

'Oh, some time ago,' came the off-hand answer. 'Early this week. Monday or Tuesday. To tell you the truth, I was glad to get him off my hands.'

Outside the shop a car drew up and blew its horn.

'There's the taxi to take me home!' Mrs Higham announced. She turned and left, head in the air, without a sideways glance.

A car door opened and slammed shut. The taxi drove on.

'Hmm.' Luke shook his head, but said nothing as he propped the fragile parcel carefully against the wall.

'B-but!' Helen protested. She was at the door, staring after the vanishing car.

'It's not true!' Hannah gasped at Sam. 'It can't be!'

'How come?' Sam didn't have a clue what the fuss was about. 'Why would she lie?'

'I don't know, it doesn't make sense.' Hannah tried

to explain. 'Today's Saturday, right? And she says she got rid of Spot on Monday or Tuesday. But we know she had a fence built for him on Sunday, which was only the day before. And . . .'

'. . . And anyway, it can't be true!' Helen said, her eyes narrowed, deep frown marks creasing her forehead.

'Why not?' Sam was on his feet, sensing another drama. Where animals were involved, the twins always invited trouble, he knew.

'Because we dropped by yesterday,' Helen told him with a toss of her head. 'And Spot was there. We saw him with our own eyes!'

Five

'Let's go!' Sam called to the twins. 'Come on, what are we waiting for? Let's go!'

'Sa-am!' His Uncle Luke stood at the shop door. 'Think carefully before you do anything. Remember the old saying: "Fools rush in".'

' "Where angels fear to tread." I know. But something strange is going on here!' Eager to follow Mrs Higham's taxi down the road, Sam waited impatiently for Hannah and Helen.

'Why would she tell a lie?' Hannah emerged from the shop too confused to take up Sam's idea. She felt the chilly wind whip her hair from her face as she stared at the back of the disappearing taxi.

Inside the shop, Helen peered over the counter at the large, flat parcel that the artist had left for posting. 'Hmm. And why would she be sending a package to her son?' she whispered as she joined Hannah.

Hannah spun round. 'How do you know that?'

'His name's on the parcel. It looks like a picture to me. A present, maybe.'

'No way!' Hannah recalled the stony look on Marilyn Higham's face the week before, as she'd stared down at her son from the upstairs window.

But before they had a chance to work it out, Sam broke in again. 'I'm going to take a look!' he challenged, his pale face reddened by the cold wind, his fair hair ruffled. 'Even if you two can't be bothered to tag along, I'm heading for Hazelwood to see what happened to this Dalmatian pup!'

' "Tag along!" ' Helen echoed. She launched herself from the shop doorway and set off at a sprint down the road. 'What a cheek, Sam Lawson! You wouldn't know anything about this if we hadn't told you!'

'Yeah!' Hannah jerked into action and raced to keep up with Helen. 'What do you care anyway?'

she hissed at Sam as she shot past. 'You've never even seen Spot!'

He grinned. 'I knew you'd soon change your minds!' He broke from a jog into a gallop, scaring Luke's white doves on the nearby wall.

The birds cooed nervously and fluttered up on to the roof.

'Sam!' Luke called after him. Then, 'Hannah, Helen! Don't do anything silly! If Mrs Higham has decided to get rid of the puppy, there isn't a thing you can do!'

The gates to Hazelwood were wide open when they arrived. There was no sign of the taxi or of Marilyn Higham.

'The front door's open!' Hannah gasped. The final sprint up the hill had made her breathless. 'I've never seen that before. It's always shut and locked!'

'Stand back!' Helen hissed, pulling Hannah and Sam to one side. She hid behind a laurel bush growing beside the tall gates. 'We don't want her to know we followed her!'

Crouching down, catching their breath, they tried to decide what to do next.

'I vote we wait here and see.' Hannah opted for the safest route. 'The minute we set foot into the garden, she'll probably have us arrested for trespassing. Whereas, if we hide here and Spot is still in there like we think he might be, sooner or later he'll come out through the open door and we'll see him.'

Helen frowned. 'Fine. But . . .'

'But we haven't got all day!' Sam cut in. 'I don't see what's so bad about going in to look properly. Mrs Higham can't exactly call the police just because we're in her garden . . .'

'Oh, yes she can!' Helen warned. 'You don't know what she's like! But what I was going to say was—'

'Shh!' Hannah peered around the bush. 'I thought I heard something!'

They all fell silent and listened.

'Yap-yap! Yap-yap-yap!'

Hannah stared at Helen. 'You hear that?'

Muffled and faraway, from down an endless corridor inside the big, spooky house, came the sound of a puppy barking.

'Spot!' Helen breathed. She jumped to her feet but felt Hannah pull her back.

'*Yap-yap-yap!*' The little Dalmatian's bark grew louder.

'He's heading this way!' Sam decided to stand clear of the bush. He was looking up the steep drive at the main door of the house when a black-and-white shape hurtled through it. 'Watch out!'

Spot's soft paws hit the polished tiled surface of the front porch. He skidded and tumbled down the steps. Back on his feet, he spied the boy's figure at the gate and bounded eagerly down the drive.

'Oh no!' Through the branches of the laurel bush, Hannah saw it happening. Spot would reach Sam in seconds. Behind their backs, a car approached along the winding road.

'Stop him!' Helen cried.

Sam stood in Spot's way. He crouched, ready to rugby-tackle the excited puppy.

'*Yap-yap, yap-yap, yip-yip-yip!*' Spot swerved past Sam and flung himself at the still-hidden girls.

Helen made a grab for him, felt warm fur and a wriggling body. She overbalanced and fell backwards.

'Stop, Spot!' It was Hannah's turn to bring him to

a halt; their last chance before he rolled and tumbled towards the road.

A red sports car roared round the bend in low gear, accelerating up the hill. Its silver headlights gleamed; the sun flashed in its windscreen. It came speeding on towards them.

Hannah reached out as Spot rolled by. She threw herself at him, stretched her fingertips, made contact with a back leg and held on hard.

'*Yip-yee-owl!*' Spot cried out.

'Hold on to him!' Helen yelled.

Hannah felt Spot squirm. But she held him fast, drew him towards her, gathered him in her arms.

As the sports car shot by, the driver threw them a warning glance. 'Bad idea!' he shouted. 'Don't play so near the road!'

Hannah's heart was thumping against her ribs. Helen took the puppy from her trembling hands.

'Nice one!' Sam breathed a sigh of relief. Then he looked back at the house. 'Like it or not, I'm walking up that drive,' he told Helen and Hannah. 'I'm going to knock at that door and tell Mrs Higham that if her puppy was a cat, it would just have used up one of its nine lives!'

'Come on, Spot!' Helen cuddled him close and nodded over his little black-and-white face at Hannah. 'Sam's right for once. We can't just leave Spot running around without letting Mrs Higham know what happened.'

So they followed, expecting a telling-off as usual, but determined to face the bad-tempered owner. They stood shoulder to shoulder behind Sam as he knocked at the open door, with Spot squirming happily in Helen's arms.

'No answer,' Sam reported after a few seconds' wait.

'So, what's new?' Helen peered over his shoulder around a large dark hall lined with paintings.

Sam leaned inside the house. 'Excuse me, Mrs Higham!'

'Sa-am!' the twins hissed.

'She'll be really mad,' Helen told him.

'She hates people coming anywhere near the house!' Hannah warned. 'Well, she hates people . . . full stop!'

'I don't care.' Sam was frowning and listening hard. 'Mrs Higham!' he yelled again, louder this time.

His voice echoed across the hall, up the fancy

staircase and along the upper landing.

'You know what? I think this place is empty.' Hammering on the door, then stepping inside, Sam ventured into the gloomy hall.

Spot squirmed and licked Helen's face. He wriggled from her grasp and dropped to the tiled floor. Wagging his tail, he ran between the spindly carved legs of tables and chairs, up a few stairs, then down again to where they stood.

'Did you hear that?' Hannah gasped.

'What?' Sam concentrated hard.

'I thought a door banged.' She listened again. This time there was definite, deep silence. 'No.' She shook her head and stooped to pick Spot up from the floor.

'Wait a second.' Helen had screwed up her courage and walked boldly across the hall, gazing up at the huge pictures of mountain scenery that hung in heavy gilt frames along the landing. 'Sam's right. This house is empty.'

'It can't be!' For once, Hannah managed to calm the wriggling pup. She stroked his head and cradled him gently. 'Even Mrs Higham wouldn't just walk out and abandon Spot . . . would she?'

Hannah went up one stair, then two. 'Give me

another alternative,' she hissed back. 'One empty house, one puppy running around, nearly getting run over. That sounds like an abandoned-puppy situation to me!'

'And me!' Sam set off through various doors leading off from the hall. 'Sitting room . . . study . . . kitchen,' he reported. 'All empty!'

'Same with the bedrooms!' Helen called down.

Hannah put her face against the puppy's soft fur. 'She wouldn't do that to you. I don't believe it!' To walk out on him, not even to bother finding someone to take care of him! 'She wouldn't leave you to starve!'

'Or get run over!' Helen came downstairs two at a time, her face flushed with anger, deep frown marks across her forehead. 'Yes, you know, I really think that Marilyn Higham is the type of person who would abandon Spot!'

Sam came quietly to join them, his lips pressed tight. 'You'd better believe it,' he said, studying Spot through narrowed eyes. 'We've looked everywhere now; upstairs *and* downstairs. The house is deserted. She's just done exactly that!'

* * *

'Abandoned!' David Moore looked down at Spot, his face full of doubt.

'Honestly, Dad!' Helen begged him to believe her. They'd carried the puppy back from Hazelwood to Home Farm, to find their father parking his car in the farmyard after a drive back from Nesfield. Hannah had waited for Sam to close the gate behind them, then put Spot down. Speckle had seen him and greeted him with a happy bark, and now the two dogs were chasing through the fallen leaves under the big horse-chestnut tree. 'We looked everywhere for Mrs Higham, and she just wasn't there!'

'And we did hear her tell Luke that she was going away today.' Hannah took up the argument. 'Ask Sam if you don't believe us!'

David scratched his head. 'I believe you, Hannah. But I don't understand it. You say the door was open?'

'Yes. But maybe she left in such a hurry that she forgot to lock it.' Helen searched frantically for reasons. 'Maybe she thought it was locked, but it wasn't, then the wind blew it open after she'd left.'

'Hmm.' Still not convinced, David Moore went

uneasily across the yard. He crouched and reached out to pick Spot up.

'And we did try to leave Spot at Hazelwood. That was our first idea,' Hannah explained. 'We thought if we left him there, safe in the garden, and came to tell you what had happened, then that would be best.'

'So?' Their dad wondered why they hadn't done the sensible thing. 'Don't tell me; he whined and cried so hard when you closed the gates and left him, you didn't have the heart to do it?'

Blushing, Hannah hung her head. Helen managed to look her dad in the eye. 'We got as far as the road,' she admitted. 'But then we looked round to check he was OK.'

'He'd come right to the wire fence,' Sam explained, his own fair complexion flushed bright red, his voice a low mumble. 'He'd got his little nose pressed against it, with one paw up, like this!' Mimicking a raised paw and a sad, cockeyed face, Sam showed David why they hadn't been able to resist Spot's heart-felt pleas not to be left behind.

'So we went back and got him,' Hannah murmured. 'And brought him home.'

For a few seconds David stood in the yard with Spot in his arms. 'Yes, and we're all going to get in that car, turn right around and take him back!' he decided.

'Da-ad!' Helen gasped. 'Please!'

Hannah felt tears prick her eyelids. She bit her lip and looked up at the puppy's big brown eyes. Back to that horrible, lonely house.

'There's something not right,' David Moore said firmly, handing Spot to Sam and waiting for them to get into the car. 'In fact, there's something definitely wrong, and together we have to find out what it is!'

Six

Soft spots of rain had begun to fall as David Moore drove the twins, Sam and Spot along the twisting lane towards Hazelwood. There were clouds over High Peak and rolling down Rydal Fell towards the lake, already blotting out Hardstone Pass, the narrow road which snaked over the mountain towards Nesfield.

'Was that thunder?' the twins' dad asked as he drew up outside the gates of Mrs Higham's isolated house.

In the back seat of the car, hearing the far-off rumble of the storm, Spot lowered his head and whimpered.

'Come on, we'd better get a move on unless we want to get soaked.' David got out and held open the back door. 'I take it you closed the gate when you left?'

Climbing out first with Spot, Helen nodded. She held tight to the cowering puppy, gazing up at the tall windows of the quiet house.

'But not the door,' Sam said as he clambered out. He pointed up at the wide oak door, which was now firmly shut. 'We left that open.'

'It must be that wind again.' With a small, ironic smile, David Moore opened the gate and walked up the drive. 'Or else, Mrs Higham didn't leave home after all!'

Hannah was the last to climb out of the car. Shutting the door firmly, she ran after the others. 'What's going on?' she whispered. 'Who shut the door?'

'Mr Nobody!' Helen hissed.

Sam shrugged and turned down the corners of his mouth. The soft, slow rain had already turned hard and fast. A cold wind blew off the lake, driving it into their faces. 'Why did I let you two drag me into this mess?' he moaned.

Hannah and Helen raised their eyebrows but said nothing.

Meanwhile, their father raised the lion-knocker and rapped it against the door.

'Déjà, *déjà*, DÉJÀ vu!' Helen muttered up at the closed door. This time, she didn't even bother to listen for banging doors inside the house, or for footsteps making their way across the hall. 'No one's going to answer, Dad!'

'We hope!' Hannah whispered.

He ignored them and knocked again. He put his ear to the door and listened. Then he lifted the flap

of the letter-box and peered inside. Nothing.

'Try the handle,' Sam suggested.

In the distance, a sheet of lightning lit up the sky over High Peak and a roll of thunder growled across the valley. Helen held Spot even closer, tucking him inside her fleece jacket and zipping it tight.

Cautiously, David took hold of the brass handle and turned it. They heard the latch click as he leaned on the door. The door held fast.

'Locked!' Hannah breathed.

'B-b-but!' Helen couldn't stop the stutter. It was the cold wind and the rain, she told herself, not the deepening mystery of the door. 'How c-can it be locked?'

'You're sure it was open before?' David Moore double-checked.

Sam, Helen and Hannah all nodded. From inside Helen's warm red jacket, Spot peered out, dark eyes glistening.

'Well, I'm baffled.' David took a few steps back. 'If it didn't feel right to me before, it now feels doubly odd.'

'Maybe it *was* the wind,' Sam suggested. The rain had begun to flatten his thick hair against his skull and trickle down his face. 'The door could've been left open by mistake, like we said, then the wind got up and blew it closed, making it lock by itself.'

'Yes!' Hannah agreed. 'We tried to tell you that Mrs Higham had dumped Spot!'

But the twins' dad shook his head at this. 'It's not the kind of latch that clicks shut. It's an old-fashioned type; you need a key to lock it.'

'Well, it must be a ghost then!' Sam joked.

Just then, a second sheet of lightning lit up the sky and thunder crashed over their heads. Spot whimpered and ducked his head inside Helen's jacket.

'Thanks, Sam!' Hannah groaned. 'A ghost is all we need!'

'In any case, we can't hang around here getting soaked to the skin,' David decided. He set off quickly back down the drive. 'The locked door may mean that the plot thickens, but there's nothing to be gained by staying.'

'Right!' Sam was the first to follow.

'Yeah, right!' Hannah shot after them. 'Come on, Helen!'

'With or without Spot?' Helen demanded from the

shelter of the front porch. 'Do you want me to leave him here, or what?'

With one hand on the gate, his collar up against the wind and rain, David Moore turned. He hesitated as his gaze scanned the row of tall, empty windows, then dropped to take in Helen cradling the puppy inside her jacket. 'No, bring him,' he said abruptly. 'We can't leave him to freeze to death, can we?'

' "*Walkin' the dawg!*" ' Hannah crooned. ' "*Just a-walkin' the dawg*" ...'

' "*Chagga-chagga-boom!*" ' Helen joined in. ' "*If ya don't know how to do it,*" ...'

' "*I'll show ya how to walk the dawg!*" ' Hannah raised Spot up on to his hind legs and danced him a couple of steps around the kitchen floor.

'Mad!' Sam sighed. 'Completely mad!'

'But happy,' the twins' dad smiled. He'd brought them all back to Home Farm and made hot drinks while they towelled themselves dry. 'As far as they're concerned, they've saved a four-footed friend from a life of misery, and now they're over the moon, naturally!'

'Make fun all you want!' Helen said airily. She

grabbed an innocent Socks, raised him on to his hind legs and danced with him. 'We don't care, do we, Socks?'

'*Miaow!*' The tabby cat gave her a wide-eyed stare. She let him go then turned to Speckle. 'Give me your paw, Speckle. Shake hands, there's a good dog. We don't care if they laugh at us, do we? We've got Spot away from his horrible house, and that's all that matters!'

'You've done what?' Luke Martin walked in on the scene. He'd come to give Sam a lift up to Crackpot Farm. Now he took in the kneeling girls, his grinning nephew, the tail-wagging dogs and poor, confused Socks slinking off under a kitchen chair.

'We've rescued Spot from Hazelwood!' a delighted Helen jumped up and told the shopkeeper.

'*Temp-or-air-air-ar-ily!*' Hannah's tongue twisted over the long word. '. . . For the time being,' she explained.

'No; forever!' Helen snapped. She glared at Hannah.

'We'll see.' Their dad stepped between them. 'It's early days. We still have to solve the unexplained mystery of Marilyn Higham's disappearance.'

71

'Oh, that's easy. She went to Italy for the winter,' Luke told him, surprised when Helen, Hannah and Sam jumped on him with thanks and a jabbering rush of news.

'Spot . . . home alone . . . open door . . . red car . . . nearly ran him over . . . brought Spot home . . . took him back . . . brought him back here again!' they cried.

'*Whoah!*' Luke ran a hand through his dark hair. 'So what now?'

'Well, first of all, we have to wait for Mary to come home and confess to her what we've done.' David didn't look too thrilled by the idea. 'She already thinks we have too many mouths to feed, and added to that there's this extra problem of Marilyn Higham not liking anyone to interfere in her business.'

'But Mum won't mind when she sees how well Spot's settled in!' Helen protested.

'. . . Will she?' Hannah was less certain.

Their dad shook his head as he showed Luke and Sam to the door. 'Let's wait and see.'

Which meant, 'Yes, she will mind,' Hannah knew. Their dad always said 'wait and see' when he wanted to soften a blow. Five hours to go before their mum came home from the cafe. A glance at the clock told her to make the most of the playing time they had with Spot.

'I'll call Marilyn Higham,' Mary said quietly. It was half-past six in the evening. The rain had stopped, but it was damp outside and already growing dark.

Helen stared at Spot snuggled up beside Speckle in the basket by the stove. *He's happy!* she said to herself. *Probably for the first time in his life, he's a one hundred per cent, totally, completely happy dog!*

The pup lay eyes closed, head resting on his front paws, snoozing.

Her mother picked up the phone, dialled and waited.

Don't answer! Hannah prayed. *Please don't let anyone pick up the phone!*

'No reply.' Mary replaced the receiver.

Hannah let out a loud sigh of relief.

'She went away. She deserted Spot,' Helen insisted. 'We were there in the shop when she told Luke.'

Their mother thought even harder than before. 'Unless she was lying,' Mary pointed out. 'You say

73

she lied about getting rid of Spot. So who's to say she didn't lie about going away?'

'Why would she do that?' Helen didn't want to believe any version of the story except her own. She wanted Mrs Higham to be on her way to Italy. That would make Spot an abandoned puppy: homeless, ownerless . . . *everything*-less!

'I don't know.' Mary turned from Helen to Hannah to David. 'It's all just too . . . strange!'

David handed her a mug of tea and nodded. 'It's at the back of my mind that Marilyn Higham is in some sort of trouble,' he admitted. 'After all, she *is* an elderly woman living alone in a big, isolated house. Bad things can happen.'

As the grown-ups talked, Hannah went to the cupboard, pulled out the bag of dried dog food and began to scoop it carefully into two feeding bowls. What sort of trouble? What sort of 'bad things', she wondered as she poured hot water from the kettle over the biscuits.

At the sound of the scoop delving into the bag of food, Speckle opened one eye. He yawned and stretched, nudging with his nose at Spot fast asleep beside him. *Supper!*

By the time the bowls were on the floor, the two dogs were awake, ready and waiting.

'Unfortunately, I don't see what else we can do,' David was saying. 'As far as we could see, there was no one at the house, and the puppy definitely needed taking care of.'

Hannah watched as Speckle tucked into his supper. She saw Spot sniff gingerly, take a few bites, then turn away. 'What's wrong? Don't you like it?' she coaxed, bending to push the dish towards him again.

'. . . For the time being, I agree, we have to look after Spot,' Mary said to David, all the while keeping a thoughtful eye on the puppy. 'But I'm not happy.'

'Me neither,' David confessed.

'. . . Don't force him, Hannah.' Helen sounded edgy. 'Spot obviously isn't hungry.'

'Why not?' Hannah had never heard of a healthy puppy not wanting his supper. Yet Spot had turned away and gone quietly back to the basket, head hanging, tail drooping. 'You don't think he's moping?'

'Of course not!' Helen refused to listen. She began her most un-favourite job of washing the dishes, without being asked.

Hannah backed towards the sink after her. 'Maybe he's homesick!' she whispered.

But Helen gave her a look that could have killed. Her brown eyes shot sparks of anger, her face flushed bright red. 'Rubbish!' she hissed.

Hannah pressed on regardless. 'And maybe Mum and Dad are right; Mrs Higham could be in trouble.'

Helen glared. 'Look, forget it. She's just a weird woman who dumped her puppy!' Determined to be right, she washed up furiously and spelt it out for Hannah one more time. 'Marilyn Higham is a mad artist. She packed her bags and went to Italy. End of story!'

Seven

Next morning, on the first real day of looking after Spot, Helen and Hannah took him for a walk.

'The first day of the rest of your life!' Helen promised the little pup as she clipped Speckle's old lead on to his red collar. 'Long walks in the countryside, open spaces, fresh air, people to play with. Freedom!'

'He didn't eat much breakfast,' Hannah sighed as they set off from Home Farm across country, taking the short-cut towards Doveton village. She had Speckle, Helen had Spot. Together they waved goodbye to their mum and dad.

'So?'

'So, I'm worried about him.' Hannah had had a sleepless night, tossing and turning as she thought about the mystery of Mrs Higham's sudden departure. And this morning she was sure that Spot wasn't his usual lively self. His tail didn't wag as much when she crept downstairs early to greet him, he wasn't the bundle of bouncing, leaping, licking energy that he had been up till now.

'What's new?' Helen shrugged it off. 'You worry too much, Hann, you know that? Spot's fine. He's having a great time, aren't you, Spot?'

The puppy looked up at her as he trotted on to the main street. His long, thin tail drooped a little, his head hung low. But he'd been stepping out bravely to keep up with long-legged Speckle.

'Watch out!' A stern voice interrupted. 'Look where you're going, can't you?'

Hannah and Speckle stepped to one side to let Mr Winter and Puppy, his snappy Cairn terrier, go by. The retired head-teacher tutted and grumbled.

'Come along, Puppy; never mind these people and their unruly dogs blocking the path. It's perfectly all right, they won't harm you!' Dragging his growling dog along, the old man with the clipped white moustache and bushy eyebrows bustled by.

' "Unruly dogs"! ' Hannah looked down at Speckle, who sat obediently as always.

Helen grinned behind Mr Winter's back. ' "Young people today!" ' she mimicked. ' "No manners. It's a disgrace!" '

Hannah giggled.

Puppy heard and turned to snap.

'Come along, Puppy. Take no notice!' His owner strode on, past the gate to the village cricket ground, where Sam Lawson stood watching Luke Martin mow the grass.

'Boo!' Sam jumped out in front of the twins and their dogs, flapping his arms and pulling a face.

'Hi, Sam,' Helen said, matter-of-fact. She stooped to pick Spot up and let him see over the hawthorn hedge.

Sam shrugged, then climbed the gate to sit on it. 'Please yourself. Hey, Uncle Luke!' he called above the roar of the motor mower's engine. 'Here are the twins, walking their new puppy. Come and look!'

The shopkeeper nodded and waved. He drove the mower closer, cut off the engine and climbed down.

'Just the people I wanted to see, as a matter of fact,' he told Helen and Hannah.

'Do you like him?' Helen held Spot up proudly to let Luke reach over the gate and stroke him. 'He's great, isn't he? I tried to count his spots. He's got seventeen on his face, and more than a hundred over the rest of his body. Only he wriggles so much it's hard to count!'

'Yes, he's cute,' Luke agreed with a brief smile. 'But listen, I was going to give your mum and dad a call as soon as I'd finished mowing the pitch. It's the last cut of the year, so I have to do it properly.'

Pausing to glance over his shoulder at the smooth green field, he turned back with a serious look in his dark grey eyes. 'I had a visit from Simon Wood just now.'

'Who's Simon Wood?' Sam demanded before Helen and Hannah had time to react.

'Marilyn Higham's son,' Luke reminded them. 'Wood is Marilyn's married name. She uses Higham for her work, since that was the name she made her reputation with.'

Slowly Hannah nodded. 'I remember her son. We saw him outside her house once. Why did he come to see you?'

'He was looking for his mother. Apparently he's been worried about her recently, and though they don't get on because of this big family feud I told you about, he felt he ought to check on her. He drove over to Hazelwood yesterday lunchtime, only to find the door open and the whole place deserted!'

Helen gasped then nodded. 'That's right! That must have been straight after we rescued Spot and took him home the first time!'

'Naturally, by now he was doubly worried. But, from what he told me, his mother can be pretty scatter-brained. He thought it was possible that she'd done what she normally does at this time of year, which is to go and spend the winter at her house in Tuscany.'

'Where's Tuscany?' Sam interrupted again.

'Italy,' Helen murmured. 'So what did he do next?'

'Simon still has a key to his mother's house . . .'

'. . . So, thinking she'd made a silly mistake and left the door open, he locked it to make the house safe.' This time Hannah broke in. 'Then what did he do?'

'He called the villa in Italy. There was no reply.' Luke came to the end of what he had to tell. 'That was last night: Saturday. It was possible that his mother was still travelling between here and Tuscany, so he decided to wait. This morning, he rang again.'

'Still no reply?' Helen guessed.

'No. So now Simon was on the point of calling the police. As he said to me, a woman can't just vanish without trace!'

'And has he told the police? What are they gonna do? Is there a search-party? Are they dragging the lake for a body right this minute?' Sam's vivid imagination ran riot.

'Not yet.' Absent-mindedly Luke reached over the gate to stroke Spot. 'Simon came over to Doveton to have one last go at tracking Marilyn down himself. That's why he paid me a visit; he's been asking everyone he can think of if they've seen his mother lately, so I suppose the village shopkeeper was an obvious person. I told him everything I knew then sent him up to your house.'

At this, Helen held on to Spot more tightly. 'We walked down across the fields, so we must have missed him.'

'Well, if you hurry, he might still be there.' Luke glanced at his watch. 'Simon knows that you took the puppy home yesterday to keep him safe, but he wants to ask you questions about when you last saw Marilyn, what she said to you and so on.'

Helen frowned. 'We can't tell him anything that would help,' she insisted. 'All Mrs Higham has ever done is shout at us and tell us to go away!'

'Talk to him anyway. You never know, you might have some tiny clue you haven't recognised.'

'No.' Helen was absolutely certain.

'You might,' Luke insisted. 'And if not, I'm sure Simon will decide to call the police to report a missing person.'

Hannah caught at the sleeve of Helen's jacket and pulled. 'Luke's right. We've got to see Mr Wood.'

Jerking her arm free, Helen held Spot tight.

'Why not?' Sam didn't see the problem. 'I'll come too. *I* was there yesterday. *I* might have vital evidence!'

'Sa-am!' Hannah warned with a sideways glance at Helen and Spot.

'Wha-at?' He'd picked up his bike and began to cycle ahead. 'What's up with her anyway?'

Hannah caught up with him, Speckle trotting at her side. 'Two things, Mr Sensitive! One: if we take Spot to Home Farm, Simon Wood might want to claim him and take him back to Nesfield!'

'Ah!' Now Sam partly saw what was bothering Helen. 'And?'

'And two: if it turns out we do have a clue about where Mrs Higham is and her son tracks her down, and it all turns out right in the end, then Spot would have to go back to Hazelwood, wouldn't he?'

'Aha!' Sam stopped pedalling. 'Got it!'

Hannah glanced back at Helen and the Dalmatian pup reluctantly following them down the street. 'Either way, we lose Spot,' she said quietly. 'And to be honest, Sam, I think it'd break Helen's heart!'

'Good; I'm glad he's gone!' Helen jutted out her chin. She hadn't let go of Spot for a single second since she, Hannah and Sam had arrived at Home Farm, too late as it turned out to speak to Simon Wood.

'I take it you didn't want to talk to him?' Mary Moore looked at her daughter with a worried frown. Then she walked her into the living room for a quiet talk. 'Listen, love, I know how you feel. You're already very fond of Spot and I can understand that; he's a very cute little pup.'

Helen held Spot against her but said nothing.

'But try and think of others,' Mary said softly. 'Imagine how Simon Wood must be feeling, not knowing where his mother is. He's terribly anxious and really on the point of contacting the police.'

Helen sniffed and looked up at her mother. 'I'm not only thinking of myself. I'm thinking about Spot as well. I don't want him to have to go back to horrid Hazelwood!'

'I know. It's hard.' Mary gave a deep sigh and shook her head.

Helen saw her try to hide a look of disappointment by walking to the window. 'It's really, *really* hard,' she whispered.

Mary sighed again and looked silently at the clouds drifting across the sky.

'Anyway, I think we should go and see Mr Wood,' Helen said quietly. There, she'd said it, dragged the words out of herself. 'Right now, before I change my mind!'

Slowly her mother turned towards her with a relieved smile. 'Well done, Helen. Wait here. I'll look up his address in the phone book.'

'No need. He lives at Swallows' Nest Cottage, High Peak Lane, Nesfield.' She'd memorised it word for word.

'How do you know that?' A surprised Mary Moore paused before dashing out of the room to round up the others.

'I read it on the parcel that Mrs Higham took to Luke's post office,' Helen told her. 'I thought it might be useful, so I learned it by heart.'

Eight

'I'm Hannah Moore, and this is my sister, Helen.' Hannah stood on the doorstep of a stone cottage in a quiet lane half a mile outside Nesfield. Sam Lawson, Speckle, Spot and their mum and dad sat patiently in the car by the gate.

A woman with dark-red hair tied up in an unruly pony-tail, dressed in an oversized green checked shirt and jeans, gazed down at them. 'I'm Alexa Wood,' she replied with a smile.

'We've come to see Mr Wood,' Hannah explained, peering nervously beyond the woman. A baby girl was crawling towards them on her hands and knees across a floor scattered with toys. She was smiling and laughing as a bigger boy held a teddy-bear in front of her and made it squeak. Then, when the boy thrust the bear towards her, she reached up for it, overbalanced and fell back. The smiles turned to tears.

'Daniel, don't be too rough, please!' Alexa Wood went to pick the baby up and dust her down. She came back to the door carrying her on her hip and wiping her tears. 'That's Daniel, as you heard, and this is Ellie. You must be the twins Simon told me about. You do look exactly alike. How does anyone tell you apart? Come in and excuse the mess.'

'She's nice!' Hannah mouthed the words behind Alexa Wood's back as she showed them into the cluttered room. There was a baby-chair by the table, pots and pans in the sink, washing hanging up on a rack over the stove. 'I said, she's nice!' she repeated when Helen failed to respond.

'I'd ask you to sit, but . . .' Alexa gestured helplessly towards piles of creased, recently washed clothes on the chairs. She put Ellie into the baby-seat and gave one half of a banana to her, the other half to Daniel. The little boy flung the teddy across the room, gobbled the fruit and asked for more.

'Is Mr Wood in, please?' Hannah kept her mind on the reason for their visit, trying not to let the pleasantly chaotic scene distract her.

'I'm afraid you've missed him again.' Alexa Wood shook her head with an air of helplessness. She grew visibly upset as she described what had happened. 'Poor Simon, he can't rest until he finds out what's happened to Marilyn. He called in here briefly after he'd been to Doveton to let me know that he'd not had any luck. No one seemed to know anything. We talked about what he should do next, and we both

agreed, there was nothing else for it; we had to tell the police!'

Hannah swallowed hard, then nodded. 'Is that where he is now?'

'Yes. Of course, Simon can't help feeling responsible,' Alexa rushed on. 'He feels it's his fault. If he hadn't argued with his mother after his father died, she wouldn't have been so lonely. As it was, she got more and more miserable and cut herself off from everyone. And all over a stupid painting!'

'How do you mean exactly?' Helen, who had been listening intently, spoke for the first time.

' "Mountains at Midnight". It's a painting by Simon's father, Michael Wood. Quite a famous one, actually.' Alexa sank down on a chair, resting her elbows on the table. 'The thing is, Michael knew Simon and I didn't have much money; we were just married at the time. So he left us the painting in his will, hoping that we would be able to sell it and raise money to buy our own place.'

'But Mrs Higham wouldn't let you have it?' Helen guessed. 'Luke Martin told us that she wanted to keep all her husband's paintings for herself. So that was what the row was about.'

'Yes,' Alexa sighed and blushed as she gestured around the room. 'So Simon and I stayed poor. We just rent this cottage, we don't own it. And then, when the kids came along, it made us poorer than ever. Simon works really hard to sell his own paintings, of course, but . . . well, let's just say, it isn't easy!'

'This painting . . .' Helen thought hard to figure it all out. 'Does it have moonlight and clouds and hills and trees, with a lake in the front?'

Alexa nodded. 'Have you seen it?'

'Twice!' Helen answered, turning eagerly to Hannah.

'Twice?' Hannah puzzled. 'Once in Mrs Higham's studio; I remember that. It was the one she didn't want us to see, propped against the wall. But when was the second time we saw it?'

'Yesterday morning, in Luke's shop!' Helen whispered. She understood as clearly as anything what must have happened.

'You mean, "Mountains at Midnight" was what was inside that giant parcel Mrs Higham wanted to post?' Hannah got the point.

Helen nodded. 'You know when you have this feeling; when you just know something deep down?'

Turning to Alexa Wood, Hannah delivered some startling news. 'If Helen's right, Mrs Wood, and I think she might be, the painting you're talking about should have arrived at your house this very day!'

'Don't ask!' Hannah told Sam as she, Spot and Helen bundled into the back of the car, gasping out the latest development. 'Just drive, Dad!'

'Where to?' David Moore glanced at the cottage doorway, where Alexa Wood stood with Daniel and baby Ellie.

'To Nesfield police station!' Helen knew they had to catch up with Simon Wood.

'But why . . . ?' Sam tried to hang on as David reversed and sped off down the lane. He swayed against Hannah, toppling her sideways against Helen. On the floor of the car, Spot and Speckle crouched quietly. 'Why would Mrs Higham send them the painting?'

'I said, don't ask!' Hannah sat upright, saw the trees by the side of the road flash by.

'Why not?' A determined Sam wanted reasons.

'Because we don't know; that's why not,' Helen

said quietly. 'It just *is*, that's all.'

With Sam grumbling and still asking questions, David slowed the car as they came to the town. Meanwhile, Mary suggested short-cuts through the back streets.

'Here we are!' David pulled up outside the police station just as two police officers emerged, followed by the worried-looking figure of Simon Wood. 'Looks like we're just in time!'

Winding down her window, Mary called across. Simon spoke briefly to the policemen then ran towards them. 'We're on our way to mother's house,' he explained. 'They've agreed that the circumstances look suspicious, so they're coming to take a look!'

'We'll follow!' Mary said quickly. 'They can interview the girls to find out what they know once we get there.'

Simon nodded and ran to join the policemen in their white car. Soon both cars were heading out of town, up the steep, twisting road through Hardstone Pass.

'You two are going to be interviewed by the police!' Sam breathed. He was loving every moment. ' "You have the right to remain silent, but anything you do say may be used in evidence . . . !" '

'Shut up, Sam!' Helen said. Up ahead, the grey slate cliffs rose to either side of the road. Surprised sheep looked up from grazing nearby, as the car whined to reach the summit of the fell.

Hannah felt her stomach lurch. Now they were pointing steeply downhill, following the police car, looking at the valley with Doveton Lake glittering in the distance and tiny houses strung out along the shore.

'Hold on!' David warned, as the car swooped round a bend. Black rooks rose from a jagged rock, flapped and veered off to the left. More sheep scuttled across the road, making the cars brake and swerve.

The minutes ticked by, then they were in the village at last, rushing along the main street, attracting the stares of Mr Winter and Puppy, of Luke at his shop doorway, of old John Fox from Lakeside Farm, coming towards them in his Land Rover. Then out of the village again, along the lakeside road, until the tall, stern walls of Hazelwood came into view.

The cars stopped at the closed gates. Everyone piled out and walked quickly up the drive, the two policemen and Simon Wood leading the way.

'Key?' the sergeant asked on the wide doorstep.

Simon nodded, drew it out of his pocket and turned it in the lock. He pushed the door open and stepped inside.

'It's a big place.' The second policeman paused on the step and looked up at the outside of the house. Staring across the yard towards the studio and the outhouses, he gestured for the others to follow him in.

Helen and Hannah checked that Spot and Speckle were both firmly on the lead before they obeyed.

'It looks like an art gallery in here,' the policeman said, peering round the hall and up the stairs to the gloomy landing, where paintings of rocky landscapes lined the walls. He shook his head. 'Not my cup of tea.'

'You try the downstairs rooms while we look up here,' the sergeant shouted from halfway up the stairs.

'What are we looking for?' the junior officer called back.

'Anything unusual. See if there are signs that Mrs Higham left in a hurry.' The sergeant carried on up the stairs with Simon Wood.

'This is the living room!' Sam darted ahead of the young policeman, eager to show that he'd been here before.

The officer, Mary and David followed him through the nearest door.

Helen and Hannah were about to follow, when Spot dug in his heels and refused to move. He sat down hard and looked up at the girls, giving a small, quiet whimper.

'What is it?' Helen whispered as she crouched by his side. 'What are you trying to tell us?'

Spot whimpered again and tugged at his lead.

'He wants us to go over there!' Hannah realised, pointing towards a doorway across the hall. It was the door into the kitchen, she remembered. 'Let him show us, Helen. We'll follow!'

So they split off from the others and did what the puppy wanted, walking quietly across the hall, past a tall grandfather clock whose hands had stopped at half-past eight, and into an old-fashioned kitchen with an inglenook fireplace and a big, pine table. There was a dresser along one wall, stacked with blue-and-white plates, a window above the sink, and a back door that led out into the yard.

Once in the kitchen, Helen let Spot off the lead. She watched the puppy scour every corner, nose to the floor, as if searching hard.

'Maybe he's looking for food.' Hannah stood by the door watching.

Helen shook her head. 'No, it's something else.' Following him across the room, she knocked against a large blue book which rested on the edge of the table. The book wobbled and fell, scattering loose photographs across the floor.

'I'll pick them up; you keep an eye on Spot.' Hannah told Speckle to sit, then bent to gather the black-and-white photos. She turned them up one by one: a picture of a pale small boy building sandcastles on a beach, another of the same child swinging on a garden swing. Then there was a family group: a man in an open-necked white shirt, a woman in a flared dress with dark hair pulled back from her face, and once again the smiling boy. The woman and the boy looked similar: the same brown hair and pointed faces, the same straight, dark eyebrows. 'Simon Wood!' Hannah said, showing Helen. 'These are all photos of him when he was young!'

Helen came and turned over more of the pictures. Then she stood and opened the blue album. 'There are lots in here as well. Mrs Higham must have got out an old album.'

'Hang on a minute!' Hannah reached further under the table to pick up a piece of screwed-up paper. As she straightened it out, she saw that it looked like a note written in black ink in big, flowing handwriting, a note which someone had decided not to send.

'Let's see!' Helen looked over her shoulder and read the short message. ' "Dear Simon, I would dearly like for us to be friends. Knowing how hard it is for you and Alexa to keep on trying, I'm sending you your father's painting to show how truly sorry I am. Please forgive me. Love, Mother." '

As Helen reached the end of the letter, Hannah sighed. 'Why didn't she send it with the painting?'

'Maybe she was too scared to.' Helen glanced round at Spot. The puppy was pawing at the back door, scratching and whining louder than before. 'If you knew you'd done something really wrong, you'd be pretty nervous about sending a note, thinking that the other person would probably just screw it up and throw it in the bin.'

'So, you mean Mrs Higham decided to send the painting without the note?' Picking up the photo of the family group to study the happy faces, Hannah's heart sank. So much had gone wrong since it had been taken; sad things that the people in the picture would never have expected to happen. 'Helen, you don't think she was so unhappy that she just kind of . . . gave in?'

'What do you mean, gave in?' Helen felt a sudden lurch in her stomach. 'You don't mean . . . Mrs Higham went to Luke's to post the parcel, came back home and . . . well . . .' The thought was too horrible to speak.

'Killed herself!' Hannah whispered.

The wind outside the window seemed to catch the words and whirl them about. Spot's whimper grew louder, he scratched at the door until Speckle ran to help. The Border collie leaped up at the latch; once, twice, three times. Then the latch tipped up, the door flew open and the two dogs rushed out.

Nine

Hannah and Helen ran into the yard. The wind battered against them and whistled on, whirling into corners and whipping up dead leaves. Behind the house, branches of the tall beech trees bowed and creaked under its force.

'Spot, where are you?' Helen panicked when she saw that the puppy had already vanished. She darted towards the door of the artists' studio where they'd once interrupted Mrs Higham at work. When she got there, she found that it was closed, so she dashed round the far side of the building, calling Spot's name.

Meanwhile, Speckle ran back to Hannah. He barked once then turned, ready to show her where Spot had gone.

'This way!' Hannah yelled for Helen to come. The wild wind carried her words away. Had Helen heard? In any case, the Border collie was heading for the row of old stone sheds that ran at right-angles to the studio. He'd stopped at a half-open door, turned again to wait.

'Of course; the outbuildings! Just the sort of out-of-the-way, deserted place Mrs Higham might have chosen if . . . if . . . Slowly Hannah plucked up the courage to follow. She felt sick and faint, dreading what she might find.

Seeing that Hannah was on her way, Speckle pushed at the door, which swung open. The white tip of his tail disappeared into a dark, unknown space.

'Speckle?' Hannah's voice sounded muffled when she stepped after him and called his name. The still, damp darkness inside the shed took her breath away. For a while, the only noise she heard in response to her cry was the snuffle of the two dogs nosing in hidden corners and the small, scared yelp of the Dalmatian pup.

Gradually, as Hannah's eyes grew used to the dark, she could make out the shape of the disused shed. A chink of light between the roof and the far wall showed bare roof-beams, rough stone and large wooden boxes stacked in one corner. Then she felt the weight of Speckle's body as he came and jumped up against her to tell her where he was. She caught hold of his collar then let him drop on to all fours. 'Show me the way!' she whispered, terrified.

Holding on to Speckle, feeling the brush of cobwebs against her hands and face, she caught a glimpse of black-and-white, the shape of Spot beside the packing-cases.

'Hannah?' Helen called from the door. She'd looked all round the outside of the studio, found nothing, come back into the yard to see the open shed door. 'Where are you?'

'In here!' Hannah's voice sounded thick and muffled. Fear gripped at her throat, and she knew if it hadn't been for Speckle guiding her, she would have turned and run.

'What can you see?' Step by step, with arms stretched out in front, Helen ventured in.

'Not much. Spot's here, though. There are some big boxes. Hang on!' Hannah had reached the far wall, where the puppy waited. She caught the gleam of his eyes, heard him whine when she accidentally bumped into a box and made the whole unsteady stack wobble.

'What was that?' Helen heard the scrape of wood.

'The packing-cases!' Hannah let go of Speckle and put out her hands to steady the boxes. Her foot caught against a soft object lying on the floor. She felt the brush of fabric against her leg, looked down, saw a dark shape, a pale face jammed against a box: the body of Marilyn Higham.

At Hannah's short, sharp scream, Helen darted blind across the shed. She groped to find her, grabbed hold of her sweatshirt as she bent over a long, still shape. Helen too made out the figure on the floor.

For what seemed like an age, the two girls stared at Mrs Higham. Her eyes were closed, her head turned awkwardly to one side.

'Is she dead?' Helen whispered, not daring to reach out and touch.

Before Hannah could answer, Spot crept alongside

his mistress. He nudged her shoulder with his nose, began to lick her face, whining all the time. Speckle, meanwhile, sat to one side looking quietly on.

'No. I think I saw her move!' Hannah prayed that it was true. There had been a tiny jerk of the head as Spot nuzzled up to her, and now she thought she saw the eyelids flutter. 'She's opening her eyes!'

Sure enough, Marilyn Higham was coming back to life. She turned her head towards the puppy, showing them a deep cut on her forehead, a trickle of dried blood on her face. Lifting a hand and letting it drop, she groaned.

'Mrs Higham, don't try to move!' Helen reacted quickly. 'It's us; Helen and Hannah Moore. You've had an accident. I'll go and fetch help!'

The old woman's dark eyes turned towards them. She gave a second, feeble moan.

'Go!' Hannah whispered. 'I'll stay here.'

She heard Helen leave the shed, felt her thumping heart begin to steady as she knelt down beside the injured woman. Gently she took Marilyn Higham's hand in hers and guided it towards Spot. The puppy crept close. Together they waited.

* * *

'It's a head injury,' Simon Wood told the Moores at the hospital door. He'd come out of the Accident and Emergency Unit to speak to them. The two policemen had already left, once they'd brought Mrs Higham safely to the hospital and satisfied themselves that there was no crime to investigate. 'She's been concussed for more than twenty-four hours, and they're treating it as serious. She'll need X-rays and close observation to see if there's any lasting damage.'

'How did it happen?' Mary Moore asked, stepping aside to let busy nurses and porters bring other patients through Reception.

'It seems she fell as she was trying to lift the top packing-case off the stack.' Simon explained his mother's accident. He looked weary and pale after all the excitement of the dash to the hospital. 'She's not quite clear about it, but what she does know is that she went out to the shed to begin bringing the cases into the house, intending to pack everything away.'

'So she wasn't planning to go to Italy after all?' Helen asked.

'No. What she told Luke Martin was a red herring

to throw us all off the track. Her real plan was to empty the house and sell it.'

'Hence the need for the packing-cases?' David put in. 'But why didn't she want anyone to know that she was moving out?'

'She didn't think anyone would care. And anyway, she was absolutely determined that Alexa and I didn't find out.' Simon shook his head sadly. 'In her own mind, she'd convinced herself that we could never be friends again. And that was partly my fault,' he confessed. 'I posted a letter through her letter-box last weekend. In it I told her how angry I was about the fact that she'd gone on ignoring my father's will, and that as the years went by Alexa and I felt more and more bitter about it. The letter made her desperately unhappy and brought about a change of heart. Apparently, she even wrote us a letter to send back, along with the painting by my father which had caused all the trouble in the first place.'

'That's right; she did!' Hannah broke in eagerly. She told him where she and Helen had found the screwed-up note.

'In the end, she decided to send the painting to us without any note, and to pack up quietly and move right away, where no one would ever find her.'

There was a long, uncomfortable pause.

'And what about Spot?' Helen said quietly. Through the plate-glass hospital doors she could see their car. Speckle and the puppy sat together on the back seat, staring out.

'Oh, Spot was the single ray of light for my mother in a very bleak picture,' Simon replied. 'She adored the puppy from the moment she found him in the RSPCA centre in Manchester. I suppose he was a sort of replacement for the family she thought she'd lost.'

Hannah frowned and looked down at her feet. How wrong could you be about someone? Far from being a cruel owner, it seemed that Mrs Higham and Spot were made for each other.

'No, that's not what I meant,' Helen went on, her voice quivering, her fists clenched tight. 'I want to know what happens to Spot now.'

'Funny you should ask me that.' Taking a deep breath, Simon Wood went to the door to look out at the rapidly darkening sky. It was early evening, daylight was fading from a cloudy sky. 'Mother's practically at death's door, and all she can think about is that puppy.'

'Meaning?' Helen felt her throat go dry. So much depended on Simon's answer.

'She knows she has no right to ask.' Clearing his throat, he turned to face the group in Reception. 'She knows she's already deeply in your debt for finding her. And after the apparently offhand way she's treated you two girls recently, she says she wouldn't blame you if you said no.'

'Said no to what?' Hannah stepped forward, glancing at Sam, whose face was beginning to break into a smile.

'To the favour she wants me to ask you.' Simon prepared to come clean at last.

'The answer's yes!' Helen cried.

'Hang on!' David muttered. He turned from one to the other. 'Did I miss something? What was the question?'

'Da-ad!' Helen couldn't resist dashing for the door. She was halfway through, only waiting for Hannah to explain.

'Mrs Higham wants us to look after Spot while she's in hospital!' Hannah turned to Simon, who smiled and nodded. 'Tell her, "Yes, yes, YES!" ' she cried.

Ten

'All is forgiven!' Mary announced as she came home from Nesfield on the Friday evening of the following week. It was already dark outside, but the kitchen at Home Farm was bright, warm and cosy.

Helen looked up from her homework spread out on the table. At one side of her chair, Speckle lay gently snoozing, while to the other side, Spot sat and chewed an old red-and-white football sock belonging to their dad.

Hannah went and took her mum's coat to hang it in the hallway. This must be more news about the Woods and Mrs Higham; something they'd been expecting every day that week.

'Alexa Wood has been to see Marilyn Higham,' Mary told them as she accepted a cup of tea from David and sank in to a chair. 'Simon popped into the cafe earlier today to tell me everything has worked out fine. The two women talked through all the problems that have built up over the last few years. Marilyn apologised to Alexa. Alexa said thank you to Marilyn for sending them the painting.' She tipped her head from side to side as she spoke, saw the twins hanging on every word. 'Then Marilyn asked if she could see her two grandchildren, and Alexa agreed.'

'I'm glad.' Hannah sounded lukewarm. She couldn't tell what Helen was thinking as she shuffled her homework papers around the table.

'Helen?' Mary prompted.

Helen carried on pretending to be busy. This sounded as if Mrs Higham was recovering well, worse luck. She didn't really mean 'worse luck', because she wanted the old lady to get better. Yet the stronger the patient got, the closer she and Hannah were to having to hand Spot over. 'Yeah, good,' she muttered.

'Say it as if you mean it,' David told them. 'It's a big step for Alexa to visit her mother-in-law at the hospital.'

Mary took a sip of tea, then shook her head. 'Oh no, not at the hospital,' she contradicted.

Helen looked up sharply, while Hannah stopped in her tracks.

'Didn't I say?' Mary went on, looking carefully from one to the other. 'Simon told me that the doctors were so pleased with his mother's progress that they discharged her yesterday morning. Alexa visited Marilyn at Hazelwood!'

The family feud was over. Spot was going home. Helen and Hannah looked wistfully at the puppy as he walked between them along the beach on Saturday morning.

The little Dalmatian trotted eagerly over the pebbles, head up, tail wagging from side to side. There was a spring in his step, a gleam in his eye as he recognised the wooden jetty and the hill up to the house.

Racing ahead, Speckle found a stick and begged to play his favourite game of throw and fetch.

'Not now, Speckle,' Hannah sighed as he dumped the stick at her feet.

Putting his head to one side, the Border collie gave her a puzzled look. He picked up the stick and trotted along with it, saving the game for later.

'Nearly there!' Helen sighed, pausing to look up at the house. She saw that windows were open to let in the sunshine and fresh air, and that the wide front door stood ajar.

And now, as the twins lagged behind, dragging their feet up the path towards Hazelwood, it was Spot's turn to run ahead. He scampered between rocks, through crisp, fallen leaves, yapping as he went.

'Come on, it's not that bad!' Hannah decided. 'It turns out that Mrs Higham isn't nearly as horrid as we thought she was. She does love Spot, and Spot obviously loves her. Look; he can hardly wait to be back!'

'It's not Mrs Higham I'm worried about,' Helen confessed, still unwilling to cover the last stretch of ground. 'The problem is the house. It's so big and lonely!' The old feeling that Hazelwood was a prison was returning with every step she took.

'Hmm, and Spot will miss Speckle,' Hannah agreed. She too pictured the silent house ahead: the empty, sloping lawn, the high wire fence.

But they had to get a move on to catch up with the puppy before he reached the road. So they ran and overtook him, saw him safely across. The gates of Hazelwood stood open, waiting for him.

'Hey, look at that!' Helen let Spot run on ahead again as she stopped and pointed to the rose hedge bordering the garden.

'Something's different!' At first Hannah couldn't tell what it was.

'The fence!' Helen cried. 'It's been lowered!'

'Wow!' Hannah nodded her approval of the new waist-high wooden palings. She took a deep breath as Spot scampered up the drive.

'Listen! Did you hear that?' Helen stopped again.

Hannah walked slowly on. There was a young child's voice in the garden. It seemed to come from under a tall tree and was begging to be pushed higher. A woman replied. Then a man called them from inside the house. By the time Hannah and Helen rounded the curve of the drive, all they saw was an empty, home-made swing swaying under the bough of a beech tree.

'And look at that!' Hannah pointed to the yard at the side of the house. A big, red van was parked there. Painted on the side she read the words, "Jacksons Removals".

Helen stared at two men carrying a chest of drawers down the ramp, across the yard and into the house. She saw Simon Wood emerge, exchange a few words with them then come out into the yard. He saw the twins with the two dogs, waved, then went quickly back inside.

'The Woods are moving in!' Hannah whispered. It was obvious what was happening; Simon, Alexa, Daniel and Ellie Wood were coming to live at Hazelwood!

'That's . . . amazing!' Helen let the idea sink in. The fence was down, the house buzzing with noise and activity.

'Brilliant!' Hannah agreed.

'Spot!' a woman's voice called from inside.

The twins watched the puppy cock his head and listen.

'Spot, come along!'

He barked and leaped forward, little legs

galloping, ears flapping. He arrived at the door just as Marilyn Higham came out, soon followed by her son, who this time carried baby Ellie with him.

The old lady bent down stiffly and opened her arms. The puppy jumped in mad delight. She scooped him up and gathered him to her, held him close and hugged him.

Simon Wood put a protective arm around her shoulder, smiling across the yard at Hannah and Helen. Then Daniel charged out of the door, across the grass and on to the swing. 'More!' he yelled. 'More swing!'

Alexa appeared close on his heels, red hair loose over her shoulders, the sleeves of her green checked shirt rolled up. She spied the twins and waved at them. 'Say please!' she told Daniel. 'If you ask me nicely, I'll give you another push.'

'More swing, please!' He kicked his legs and shrieked with delight.

Helen risked a sideways glance at Hannah. Hannah turned with a broad smile to face Helen. Without saying a word, each knew what the other was thinking. They said it out loud in any case.

'Suddenly . . .' Helen began.

'. . . Spot's future . . .' Hannah went on.

'. . . Looks very . . .'

'. . . *Very* . . .'

With smiles that split their faces in two under their dark, glossy fringes, they finished the sentence as one. '. . . Bright!'

SHELLEY THE SHADOW
Home Farm Twins 19

Jenny Oldfield

Meet Helen and Hannah. They're identical twins – and mad about the animals on their Lake District farm!

Shelley is the smallest duckling in her family. She's always last in line and struggling to keep up – so, when her mother and siblings flee from a hungry fox, Shelley's soon left behind. Helen and Hannah save the little duckling and take her back to Home Farm. But now Shelley has latched on to the twins and follows them everywhere. Will they ever reunite her with her missing family?

STAR THE SURPRISE
Home Farm Twins 20

Jenny Oldfield

Meet Helen and Hannah. They're identical twins – and mad about the animals on their Lake District farm!

A thoroughbred foal is born at a livery stables near Doveton – surprising everyone with her early arrival! Hannah and Helen only just get there in time to watch. Now she needs special care, and the twins are willing volunteers. Left in charge while her owner is away, Star springs another surprise on them by disappearing. Has she run away, or is it theft? The twins only have twenty four hours to find out!

STALKY THE MASCOT
Home Farm Twins Summer Special

Jenny Oldfield

Meet Helen and Hannah. They're identical twins – and mad about the animals on their Lake District farm!

On holiday in New Zealand with their cousins Mike and Martin James, Helen and Hannah help to rescue Stalky, an orphaned baby kiwi. They prepare to return him to the wild – until they hear of a local landowner's plans to build a new holiday resort right in the middle of his forest home. With his habitat under threat, Stalky's whole future seems once more in doubt . . .

HORSES OF HALF-MOON RANCH
Wild Horses

Jenny Oldfield

A wild and dangerous mountain setting and a daughter who lives, breathes and sleeps horses is a recipe for trouble for ranch owner, Sandy Scott. But Kirstie is undaunted by her mother's warnings. She's at her happiest riding the trails through the tall forests and deep canyons of the Meltwater Range . . .

Leading a trek in early summer, the fine weather turns. Creeks have flooded during torrential rain and now a landslide in a deep mountain gorge separates Kirstie and her pony, Lucky, from the rest of her group. They're trapped in Dead Man's Canyon with a herd of wild horses, one of whom has been hurt by falling rocks. Cold and alone in the gathering storm, how is Kirstie going to get help to the injured stallion?

HOME FARM TWINS
Jenny Oldfield

All Hodder Children's books are available at your local bookshop, or can be ordered direct from the publisher. Just tick the titles you would like and complete the details below. Prices and availability are subject to change without prior notice.

Please enclose a cheque or postal order made payable to *Bookpoint Ltd*, and send to: Hodder Children's Books, 39 Milton Park, Abingdon, OXON OX14 4TD, UK. Email Address: orders@bookpoint.co.uk

If you would prefer to pay by credit card, our call centre team would be delighted to take your order by telephone. Our direct line *01235 400414* (lines open 9.00 am–6.00 pm Monday to Saturday, 24 hour message answering service). Alternatively you can send a fax on *01235 400454*.

TITLE		FIRST NAME		SURNAME	

ADDRESS	

DAYTIME TEL:		POST CODE	

If you would prefer to pay by credit card, please complete:
Please debit my Visa/Access/Diner's Card/American Express (delete as applicable) card no:

Signature .... Expiry Date: ....

If you would NOT like to receive further information on our products please tick the box. ❏

ORDER FORM

Horses of Half-Moon Ranch
Jenny Oldfield

0 340 71616 9	1: WILD HORSES	£3.99	❏
0 340 71617 7	2: RODEO ROCKY	£3.99	❏
0 340 71618 5	3: CRAZY HORSE	£3.99	❏
0 340 71619 3	4: JOHNNY MOHAWK	£3.99	❏
0 340 71620 7	5: MIDNIGHT LADY	£3.99	❏
0 340 71621 5	6: THIRD-TIME LUCKY	£3.99	❏

*All Hodder Children's books are available at your local bookshop,
or can be ordered direct from the publisher. Just tick the titles you
would like and complete the details below. Prices and availability
are subject to change without prior notice.*

Please enclose a cheque or postal order made payable to *Bookpoint
Ltd*, and send to: Hodder Children's Books, 39 Milton Park,
Abingdon, OXON OX14 4TD, UK.
Email Address: orders@bookpoint.co.uk

If you would prefer to pay by credit card, our call centre team would
be delighted to take your order by telephone. Our direct line *01235
400414* (lines open 9.00 am–6.00 pm Monday to Saturday, 24 hour
message answering service). Alternatively you can send a fax on
01235 400454.

TITLE		FIRST NAME		SURNAME	

ADDRESS

DAYTIME TEL: POST CODE

If you would prefer to pay by credit card, please complete:
Please debit my Visa/Access/Diner's Card/American Express (delete
as applicable) card no:

Signature .... Expiry Date: ....

If you would NOT like to receive further information on our products
please tick the box. ❐